THE HAPLESS CHILD

by Edward Gorey

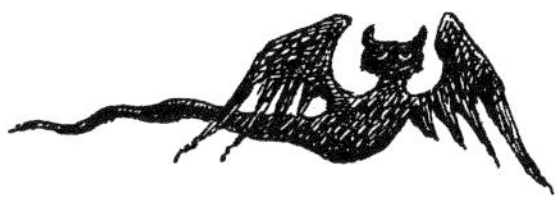

Pomegranate

PORTLAND, OREGON

Pomegranate Communications, Inc.
105 SE 18th Ave., Portland, OR 97214
800-227-1428 pomegranate.com
sales@pomegranate.com

Library of Congress Control Number: 2007935943

Item No. A146
ISBN 978-0-7649-4468-0

Printed in China

35 34 33 32 31 30 29 28 27 26 16 15 14 13 12 11 10 9 8 7

To the memory of V. R. Lang

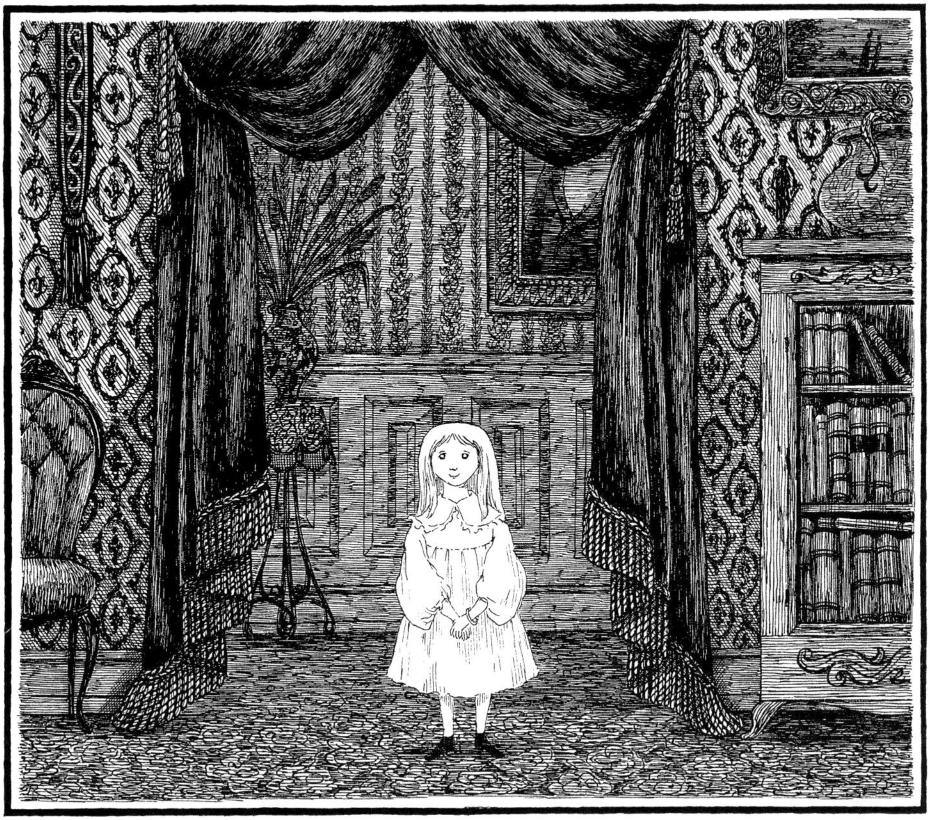

There was once a little girl named Charlotte Sophia.

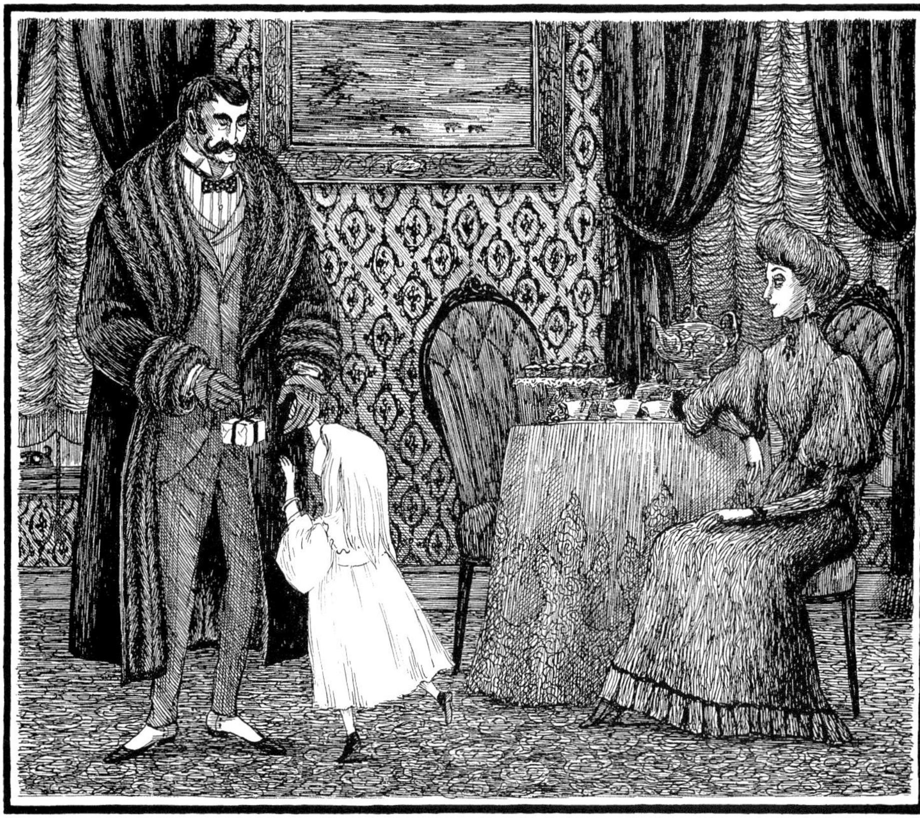

Her parents were kind and well-to-do.

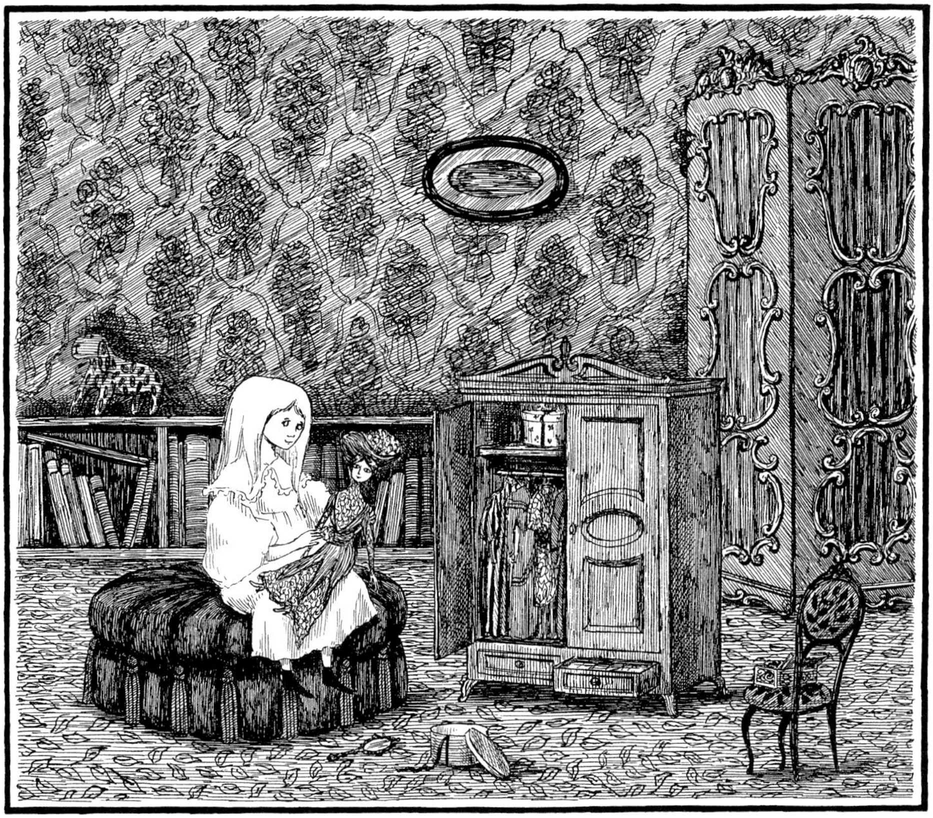

She had a doll whom she called Hortense.

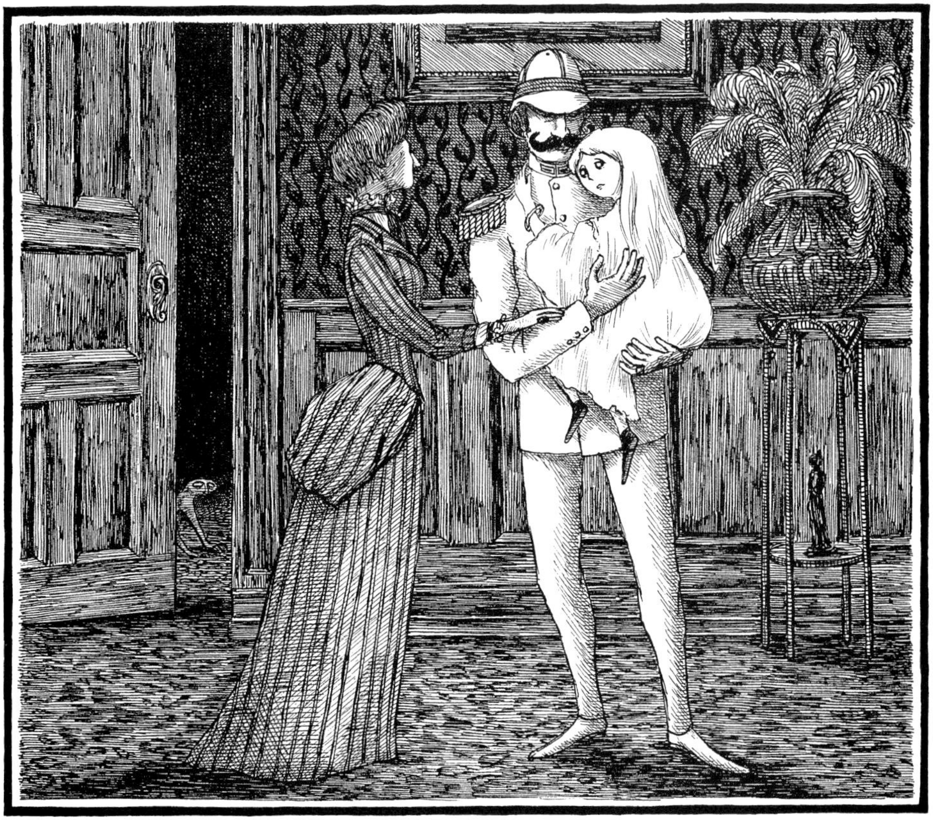

One day her father, a colonel in the army, was ordered to Africa.

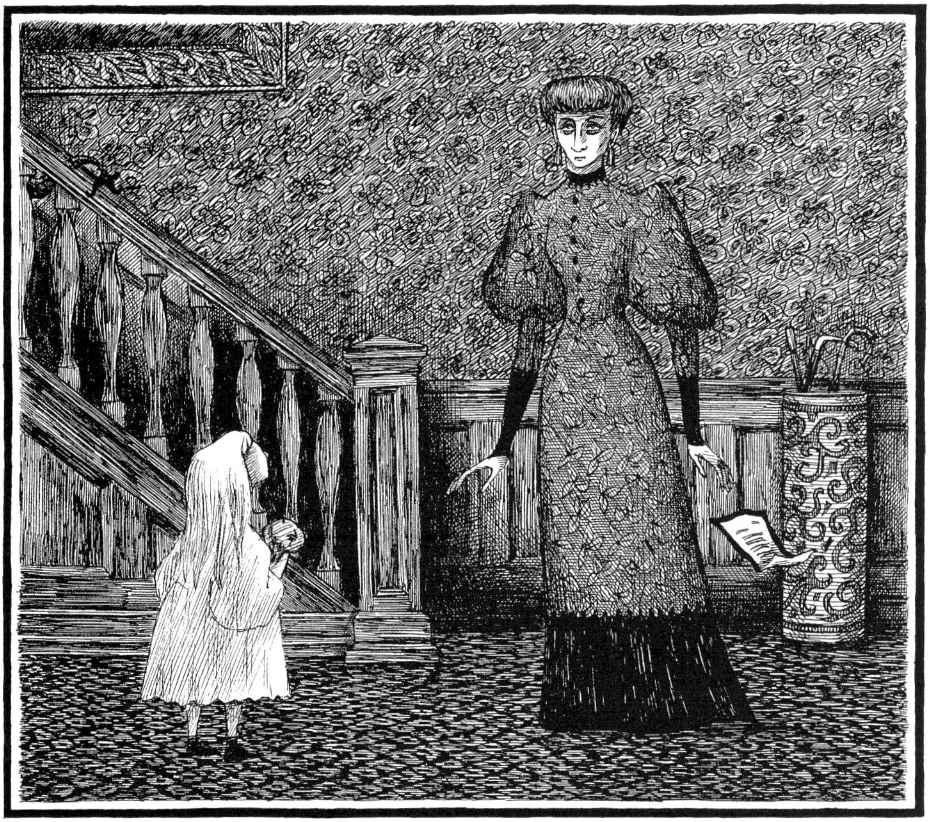

Several months later he was reported killed in a native uprising.

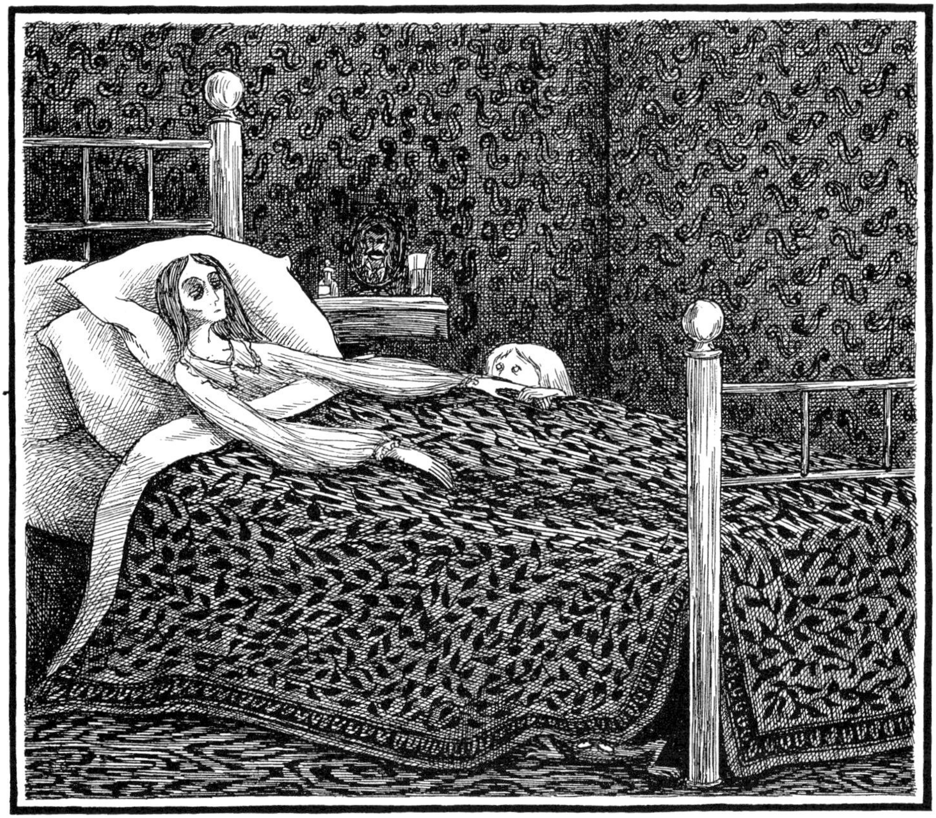

Her mother fell into a decline that proved fatal.

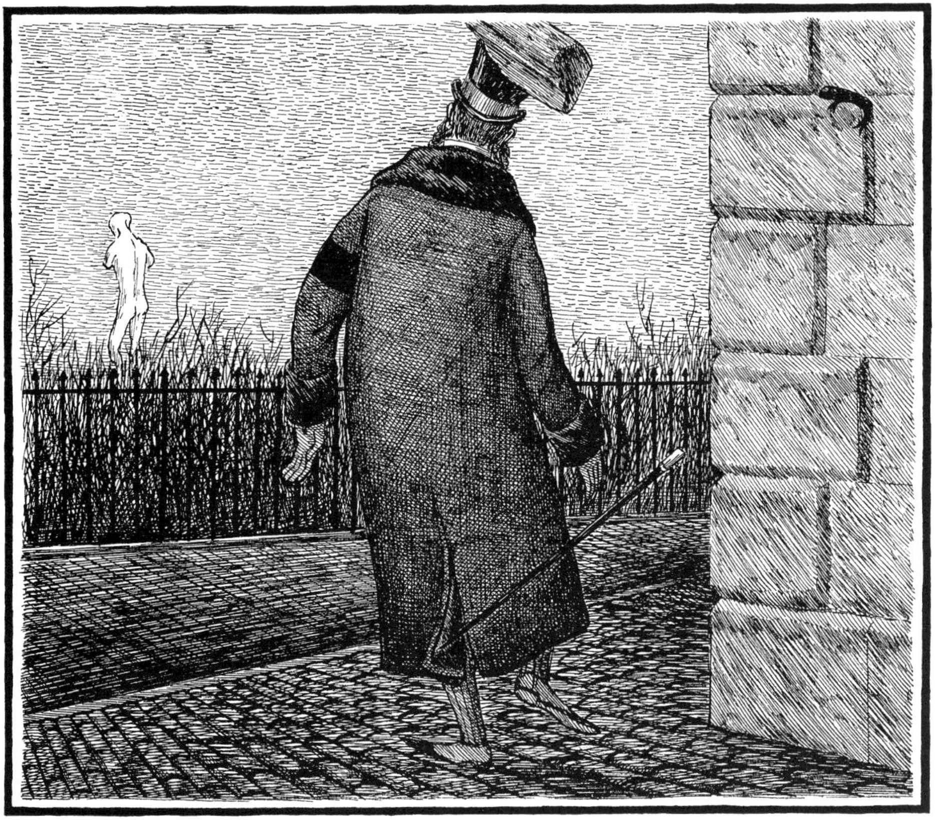

Her only other relative, an uncle, was brained by a piece of masonry.

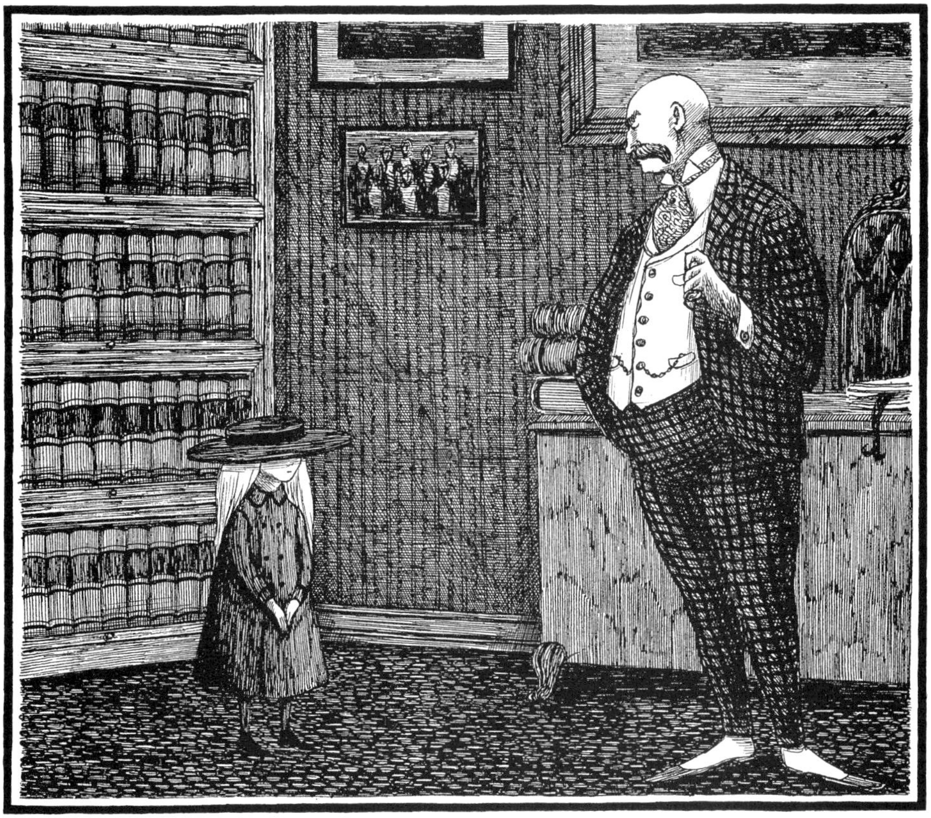

Charlotte Sophia was left in the hands of
the family lawyer.

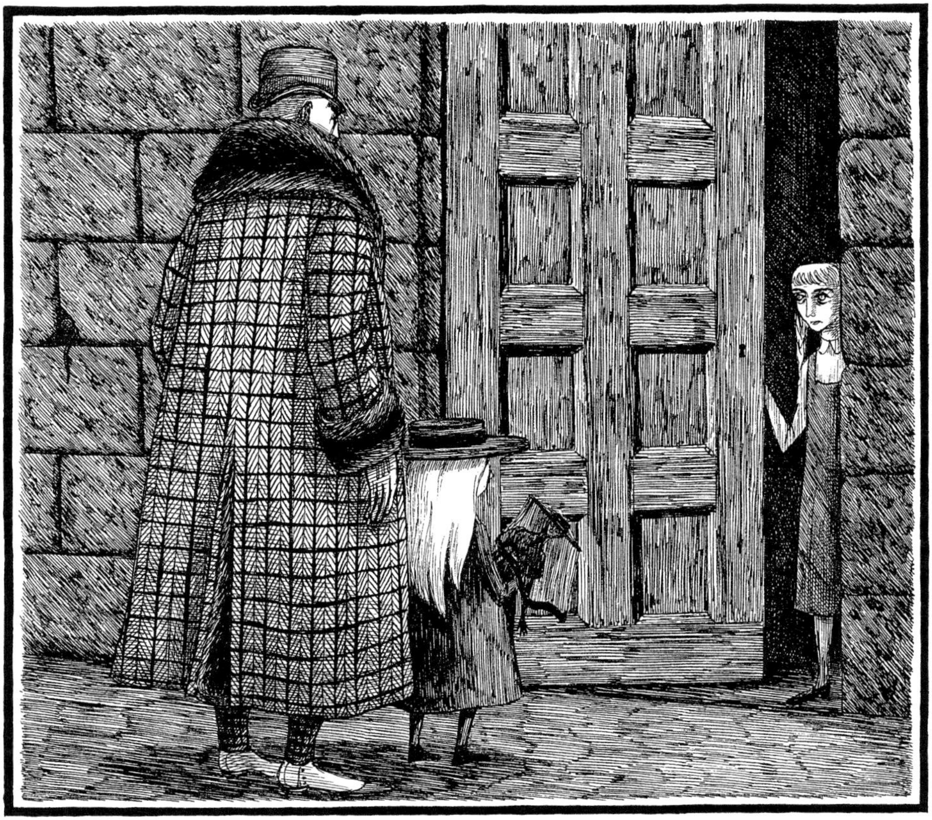

He at once put her into a boarding-school.

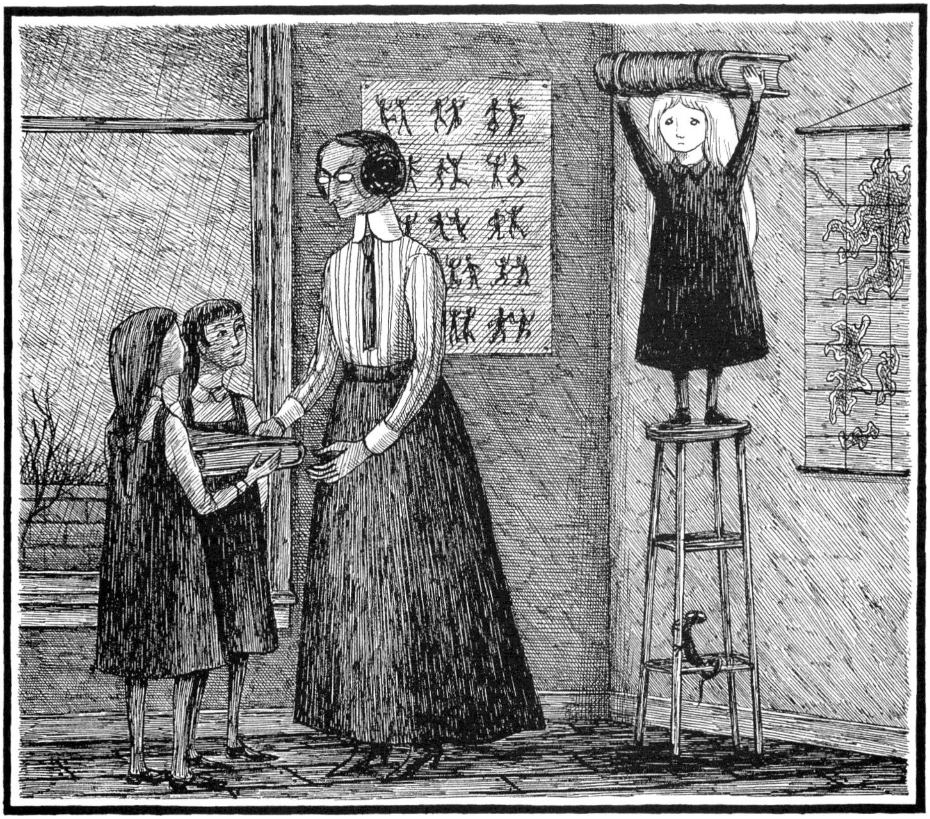

There she was punished by the teachers for things she hadn't done.

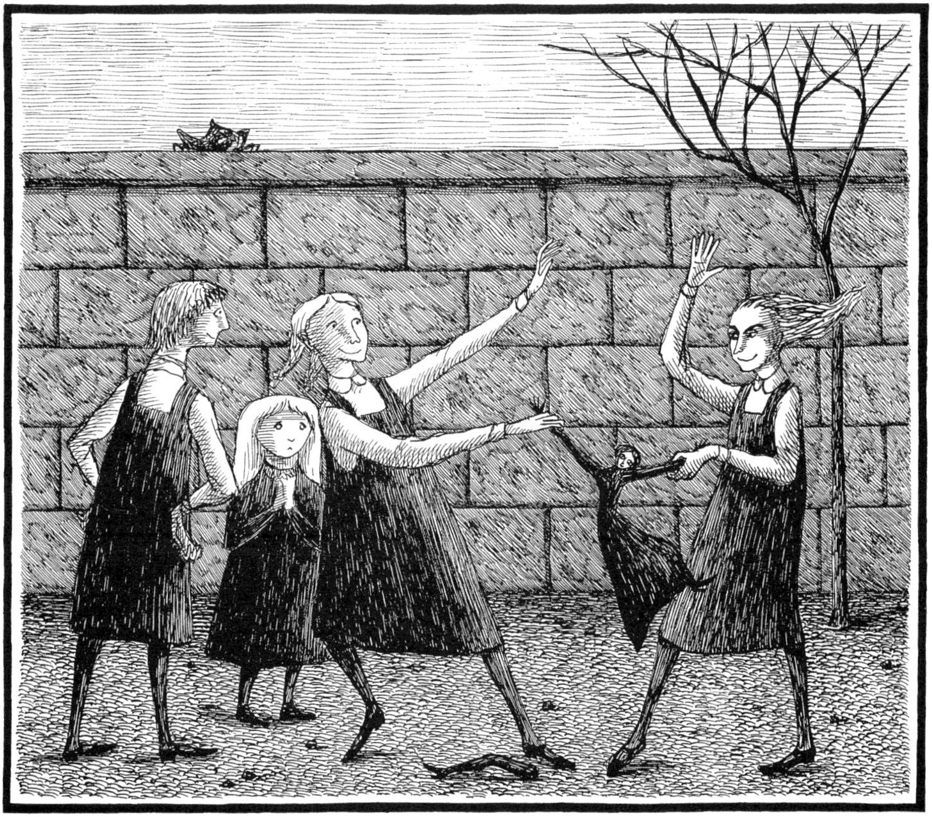

Hortense was torn limb from limb by the other pupils.

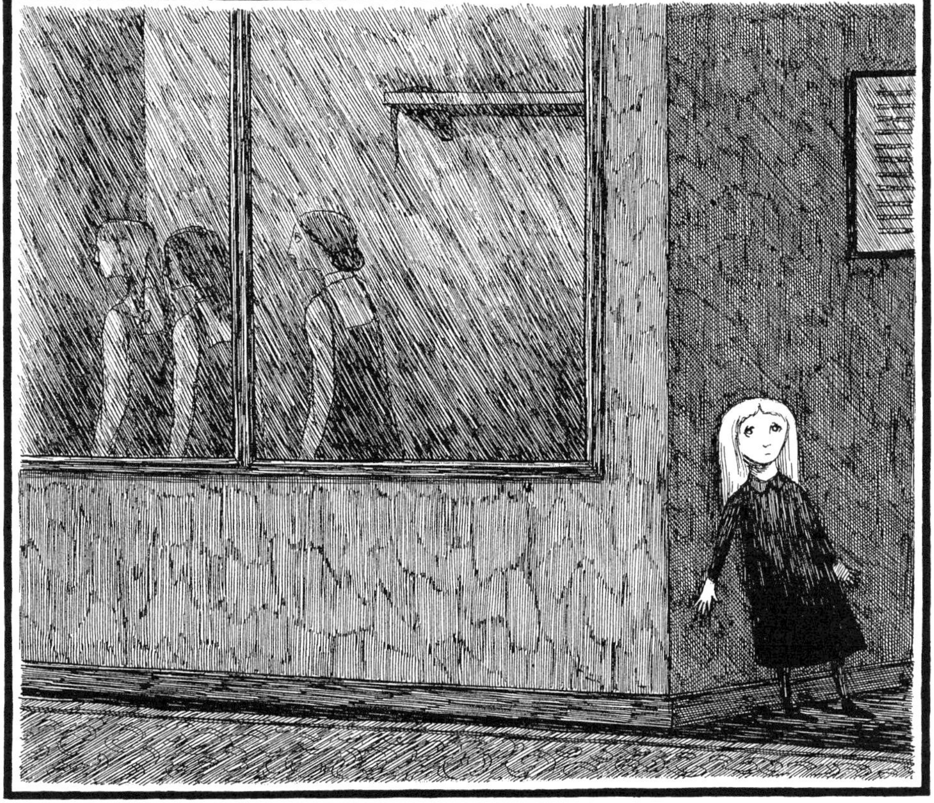

During the day Charlotte Sophia hid as much as possible.

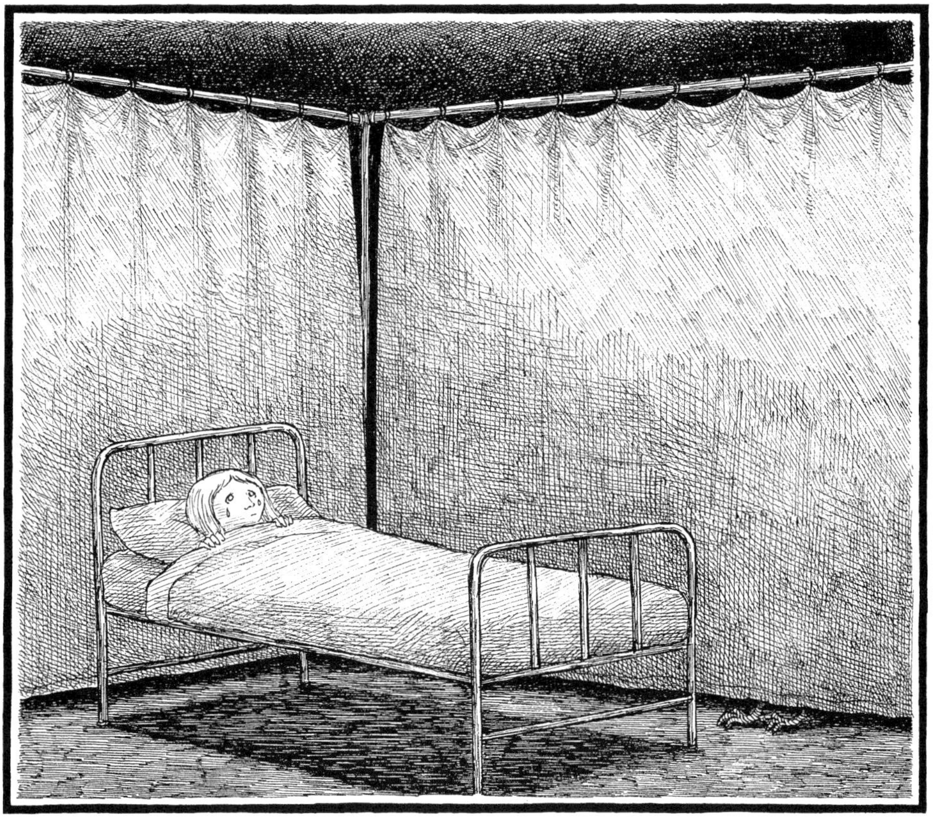

At night she lay awake weeping and weeping.

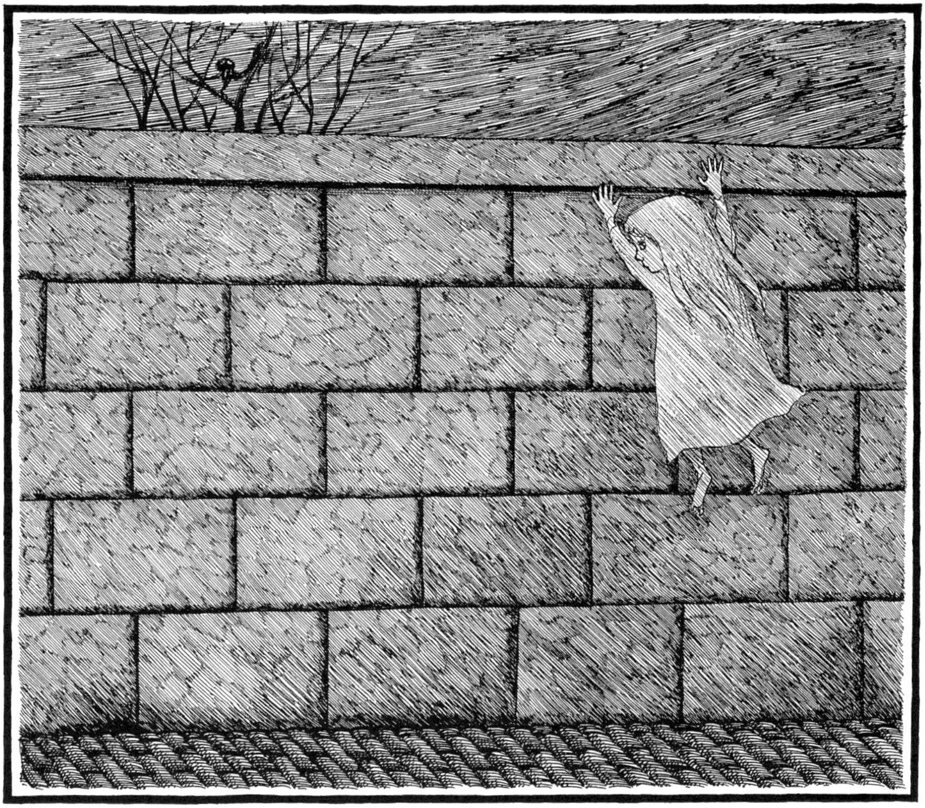

When she could bear it no longer she fled from the school at dawn.

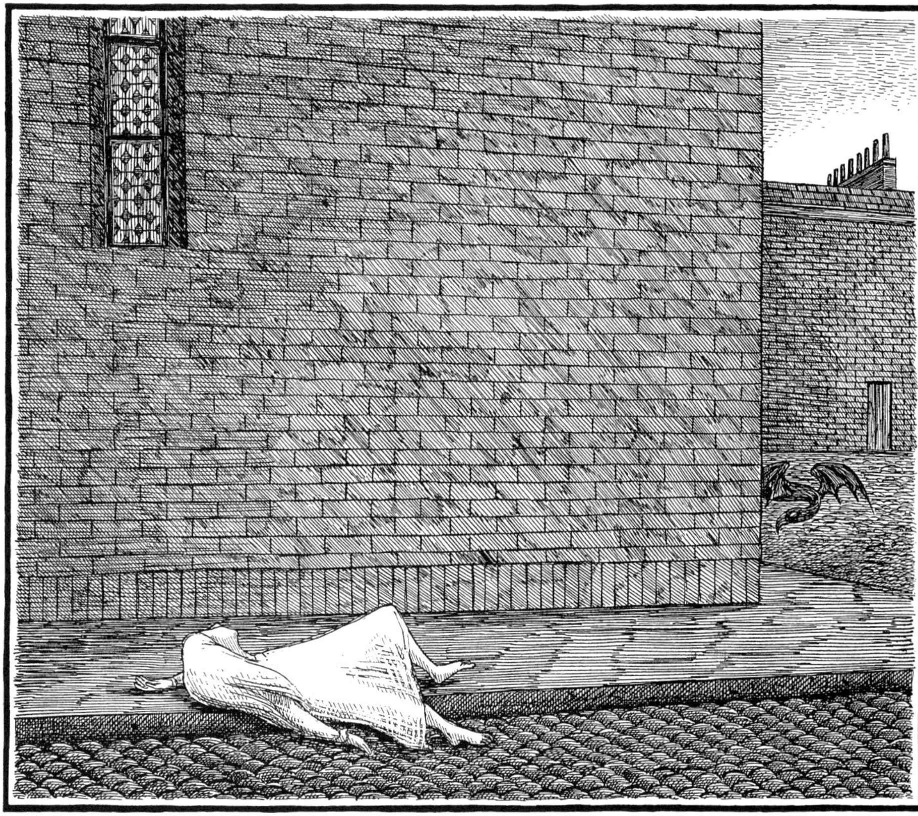

She soon lost consciousness and sank to the pavement.

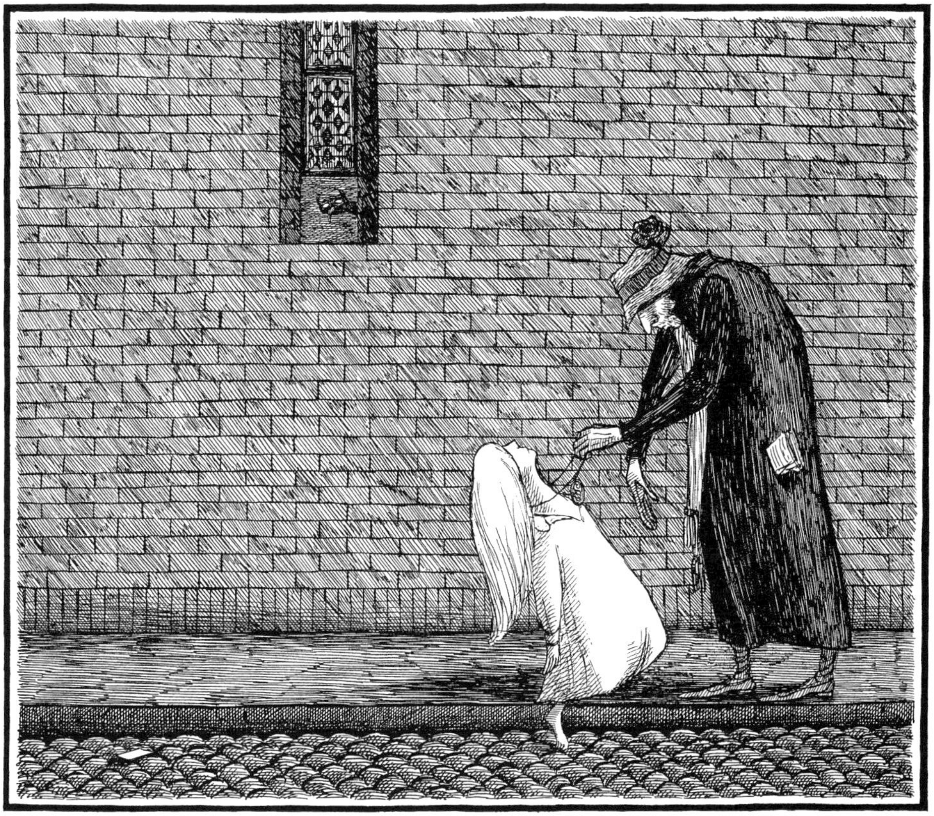

A man came and took the locket with her parents' pictures inside.

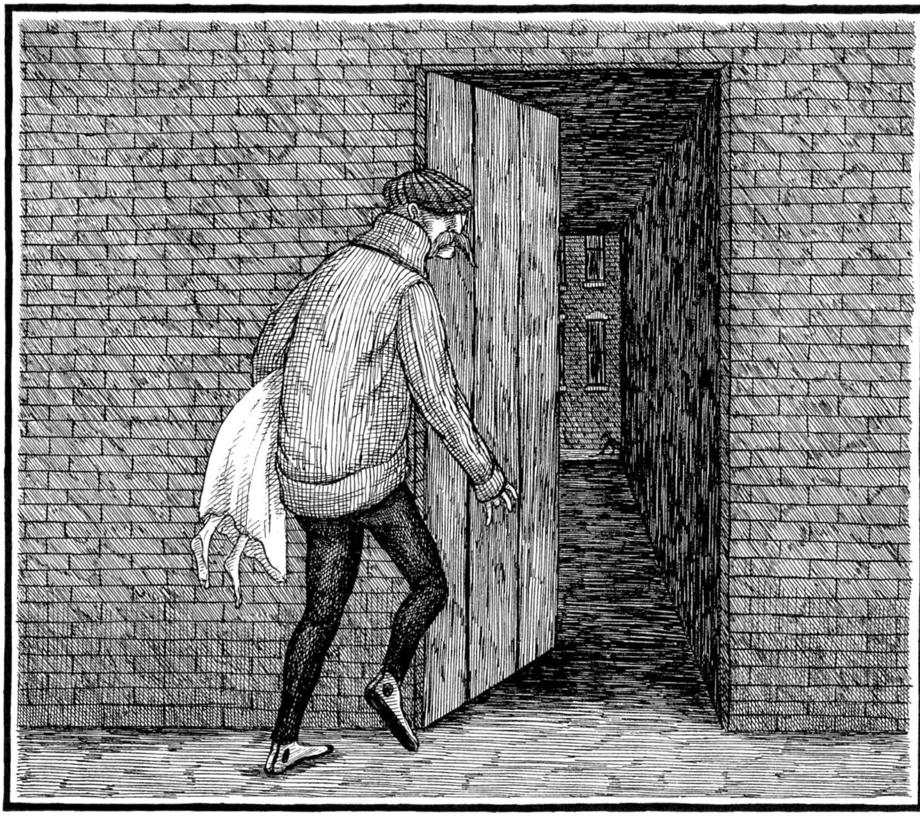

Another man came from the opposite direction and carried her off.

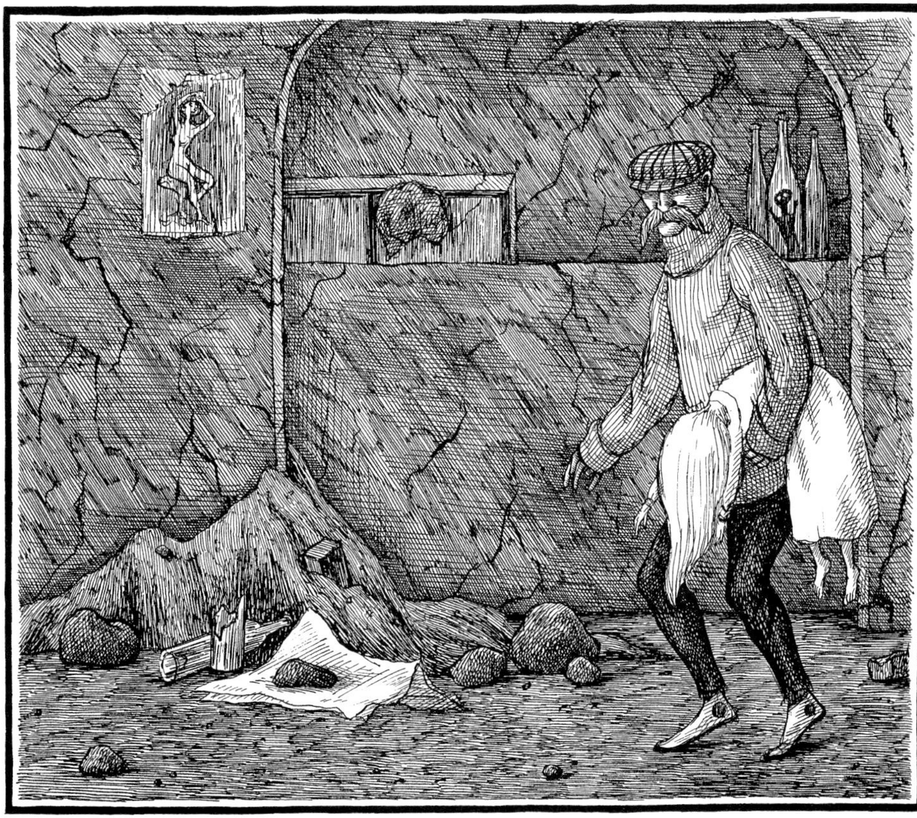

He brought her to a low place.

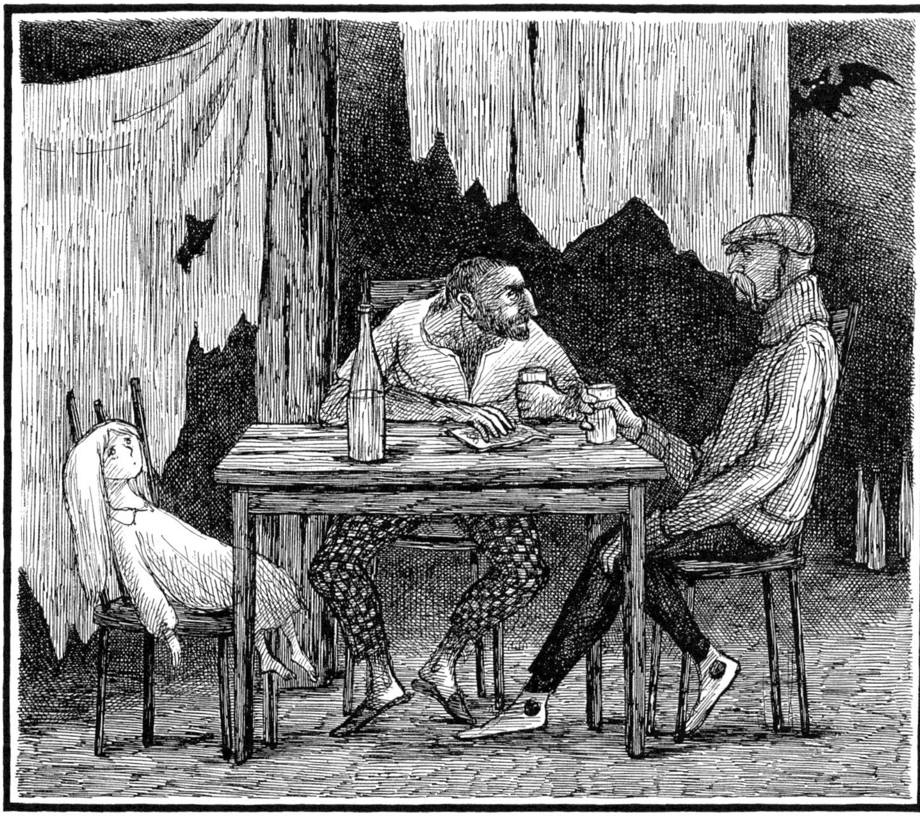

He sold her to a drunken brute.

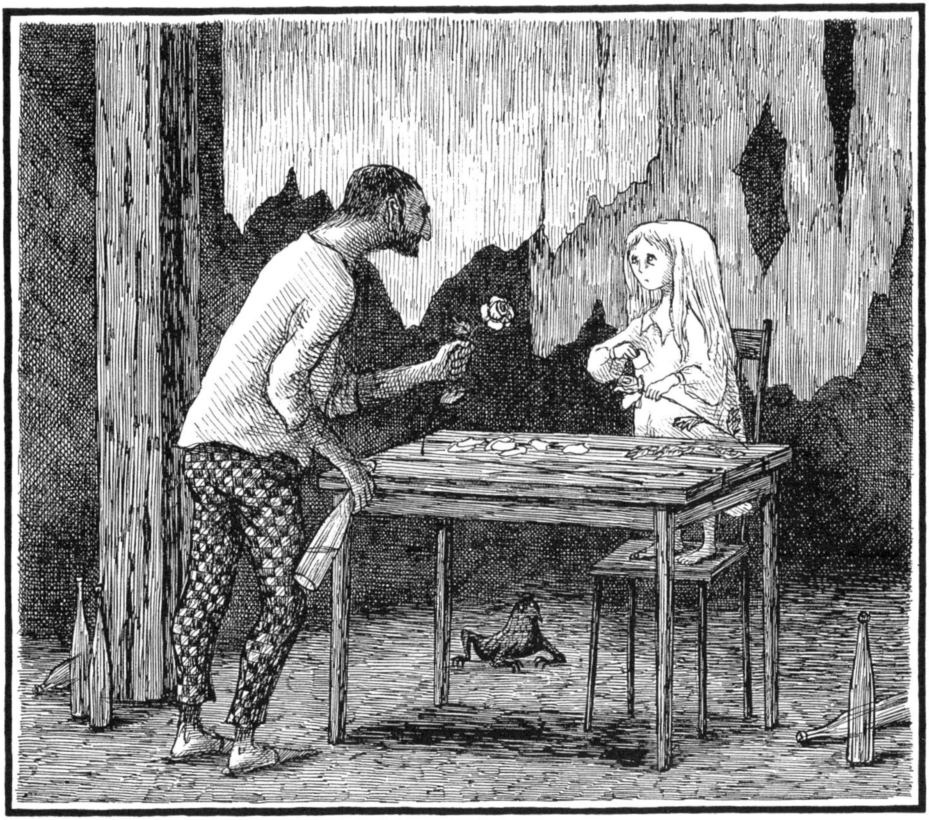

Charlotte Sophia was put to work making artificial flowers.

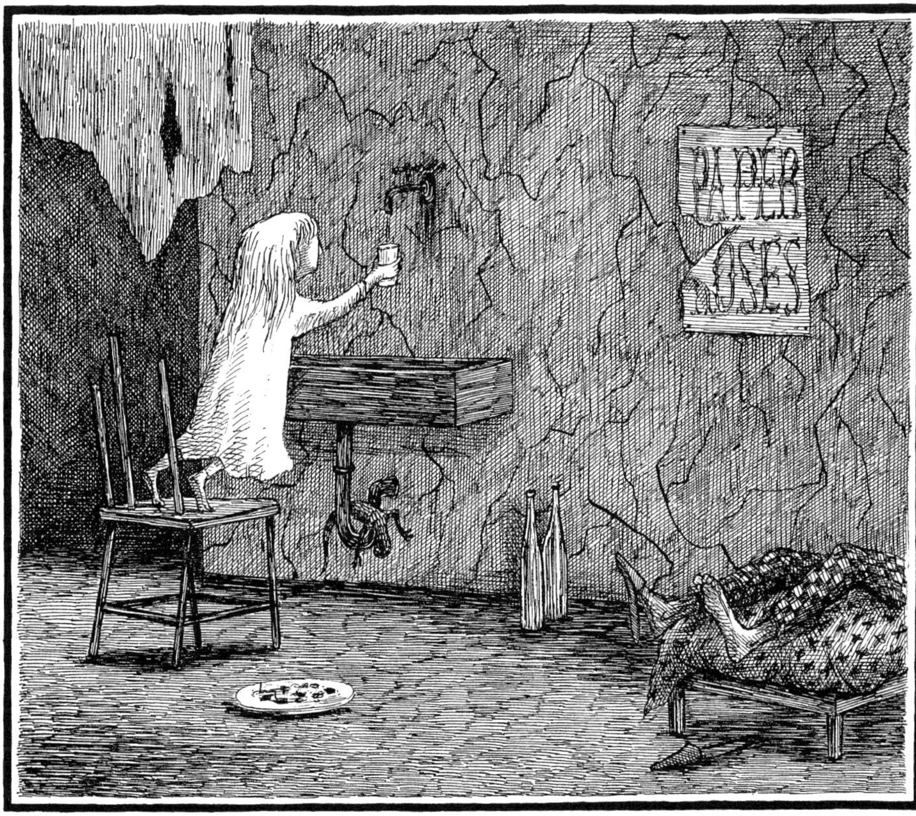

She lived on scraps and tap-water.

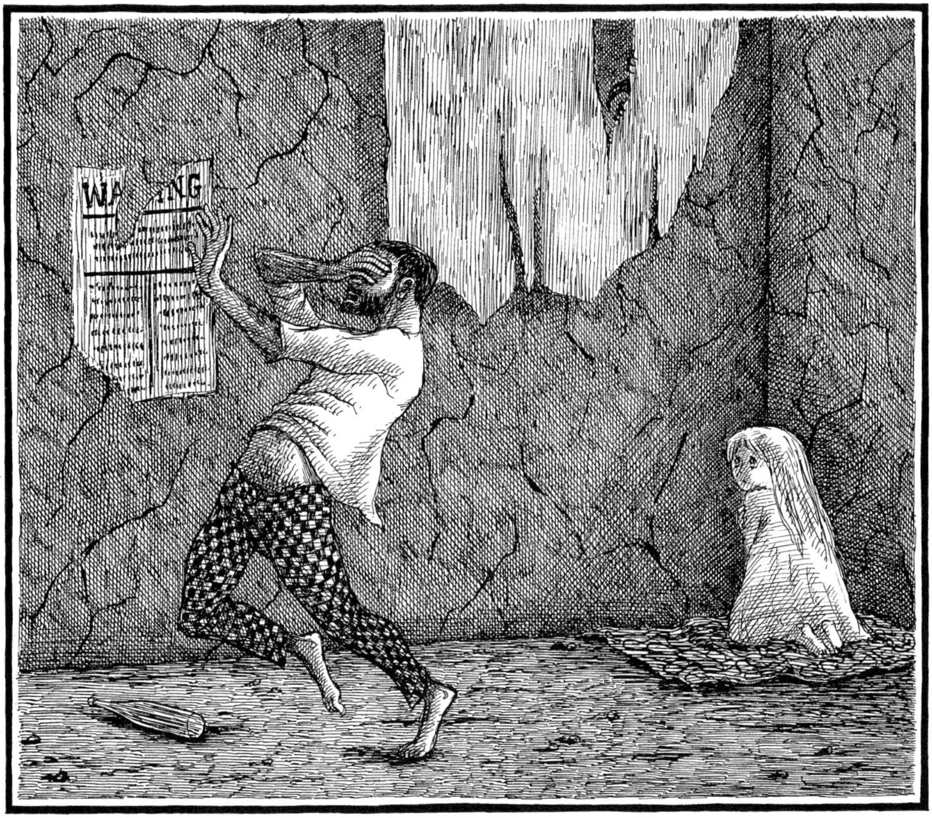

From time to time the brute got the horrors.

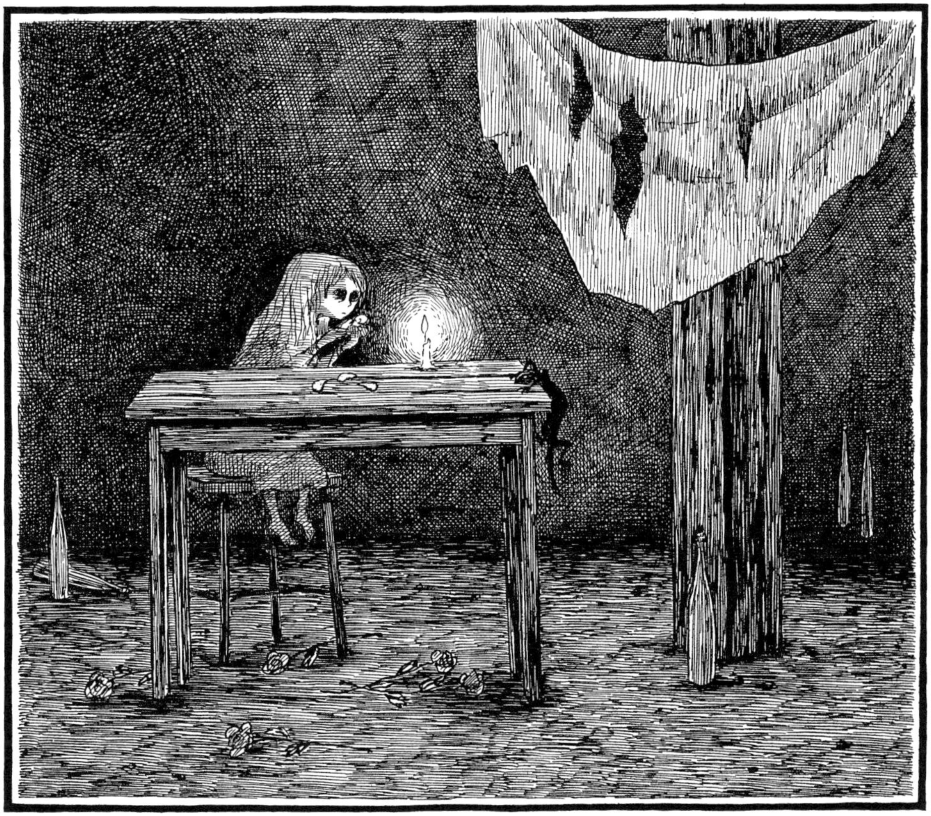

Charlotte Sophia's eyesight began to fail rapidly.

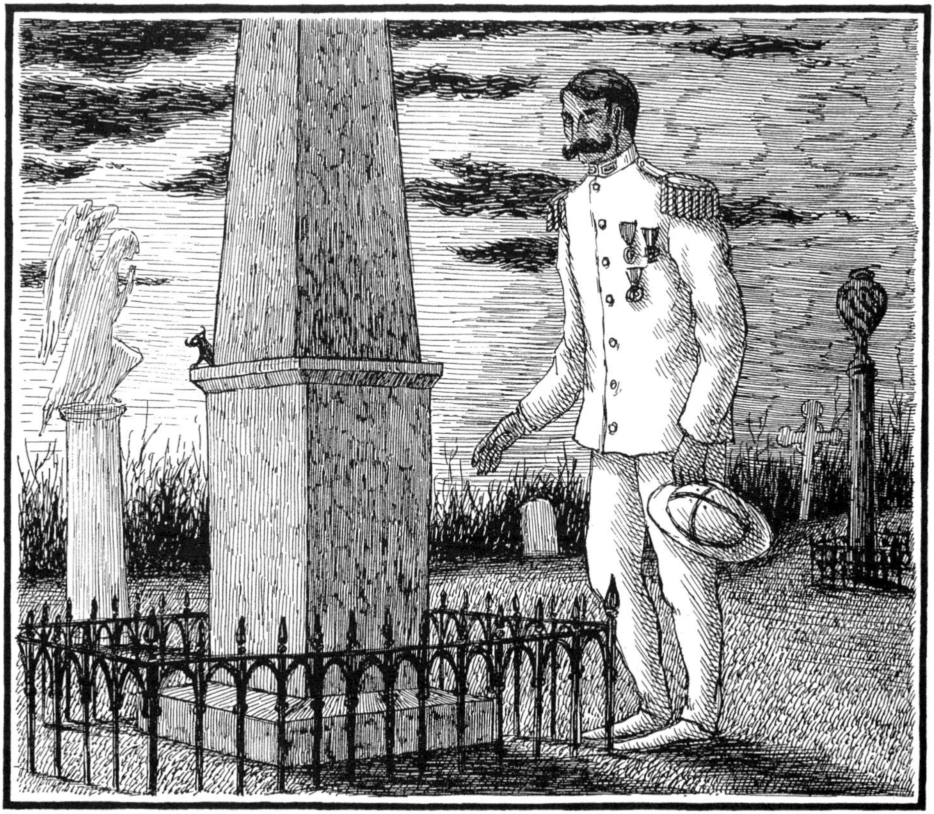

Meanwhile, her father, who was not dead after all,
returned home.

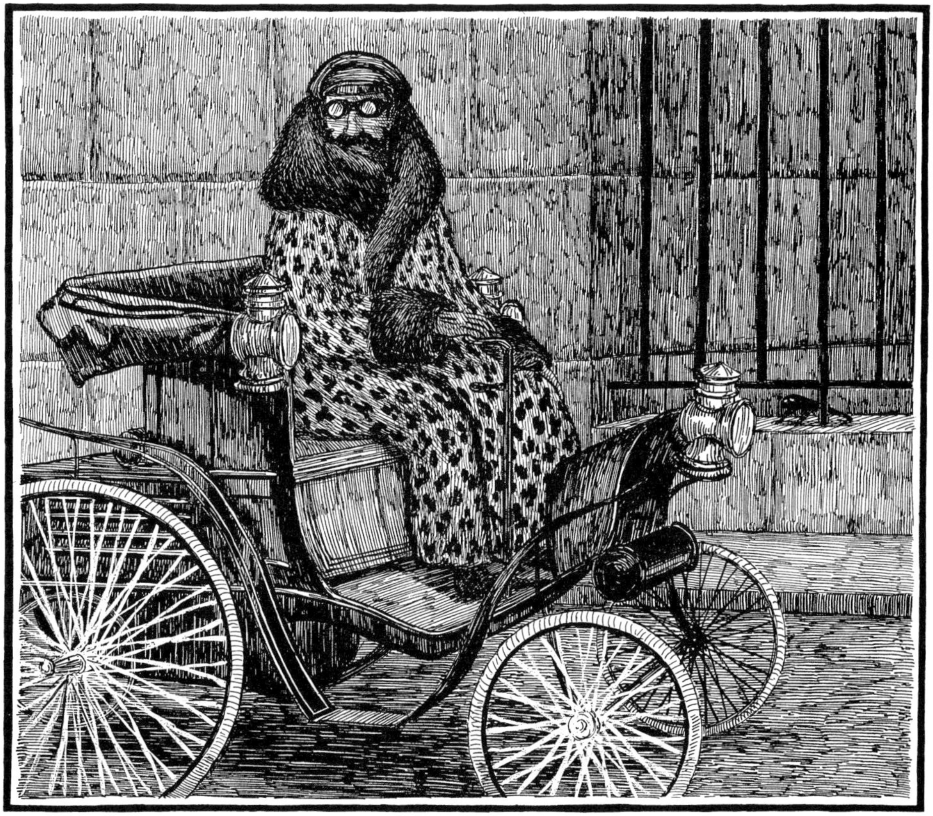

Every day he motored through the streets searching for her.

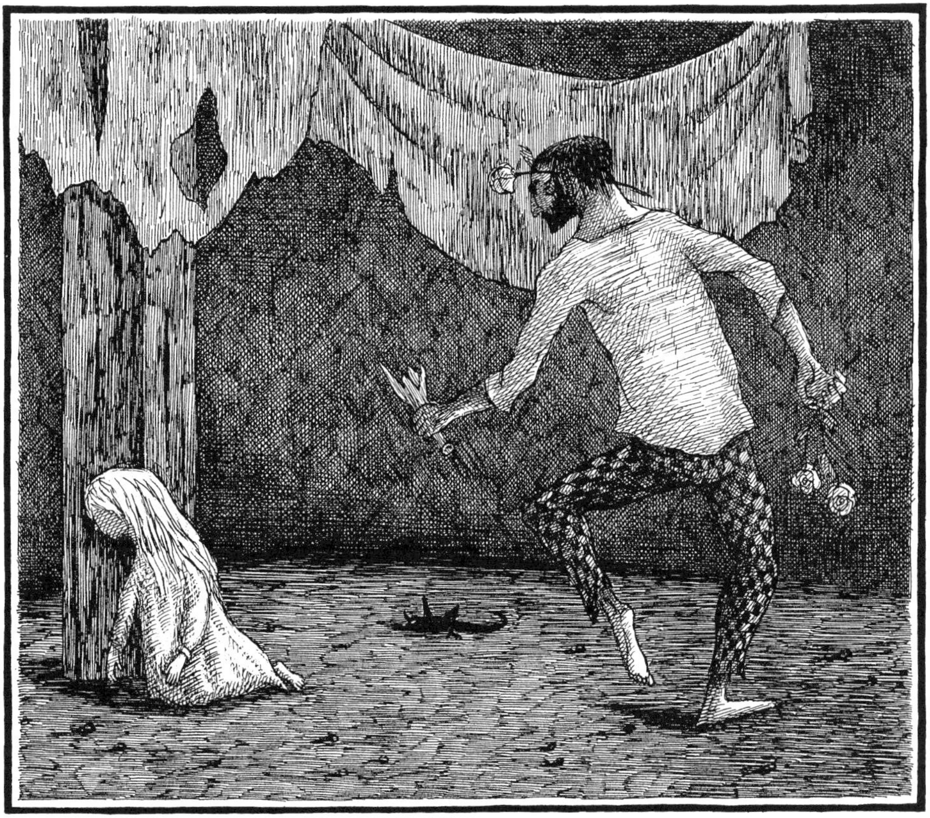

At last the brute went off his head.

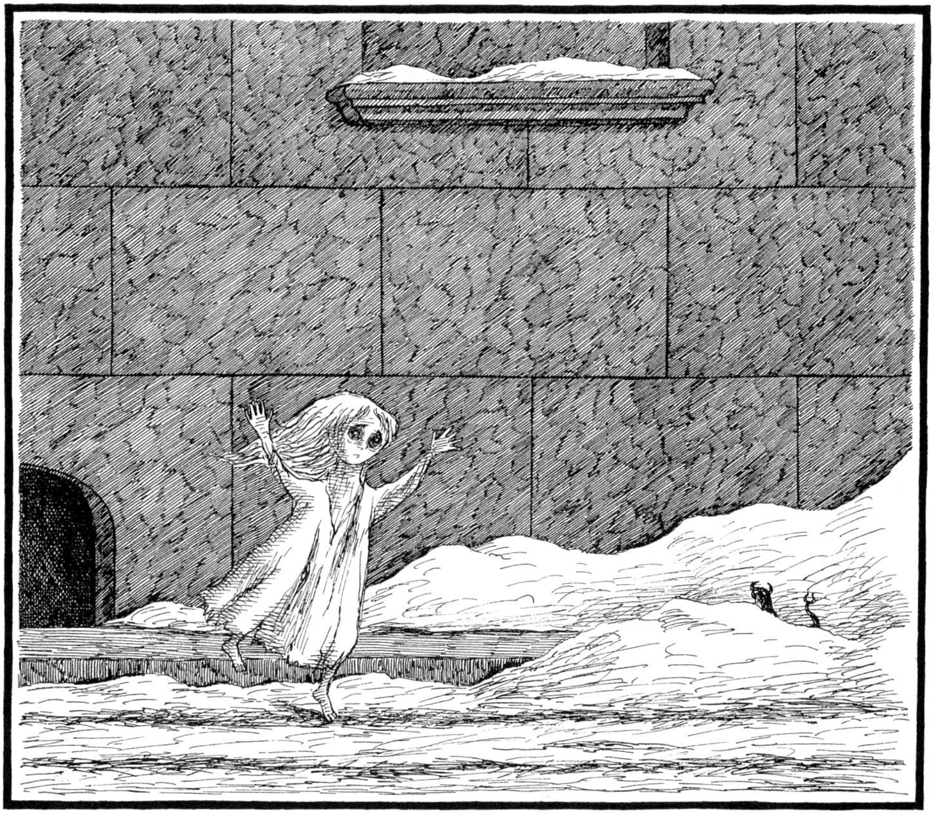

Charlotte Sophia, now almost blind, ran into the street.

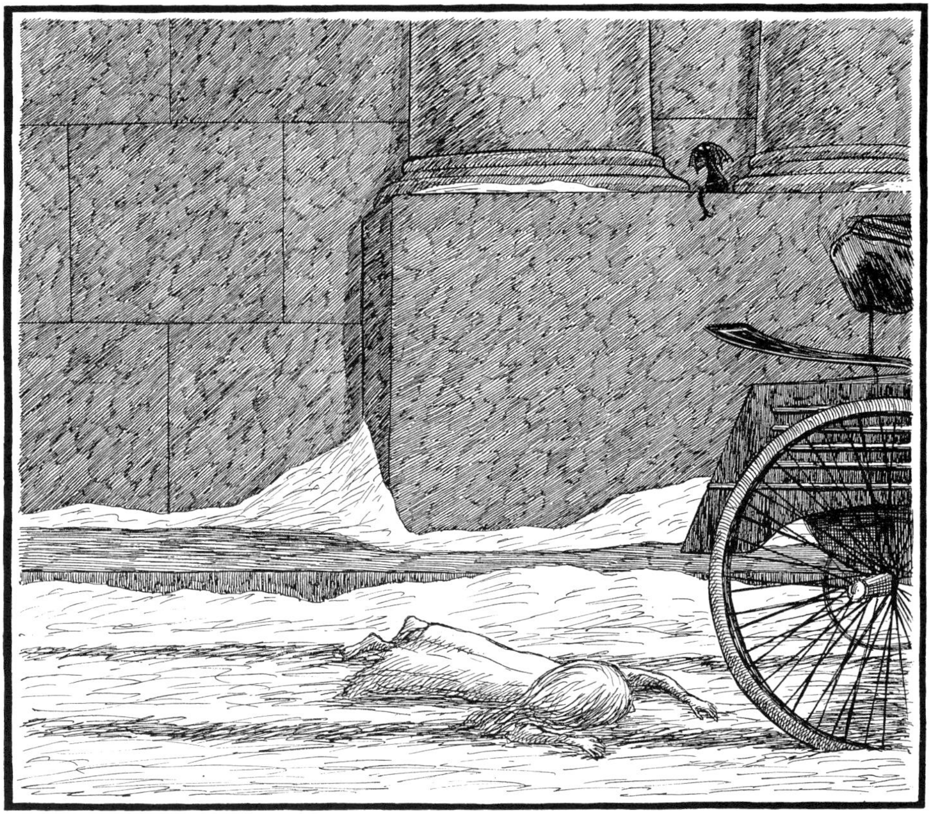

She was at once struck down by a car.

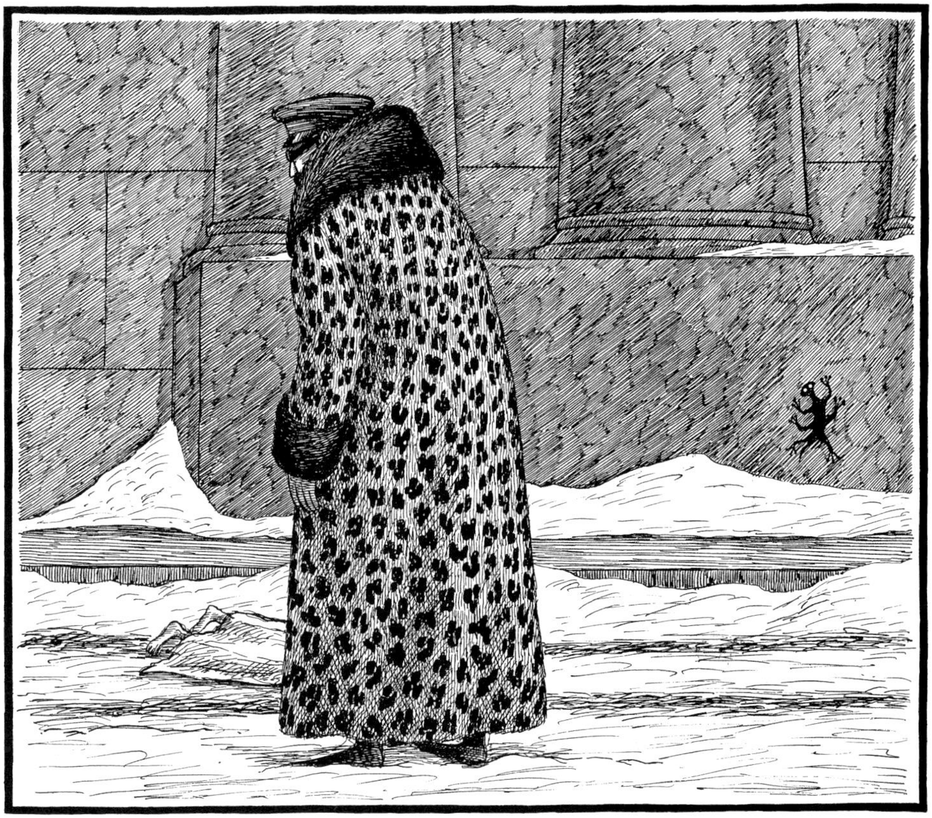

Her father got out to look at the dying child.

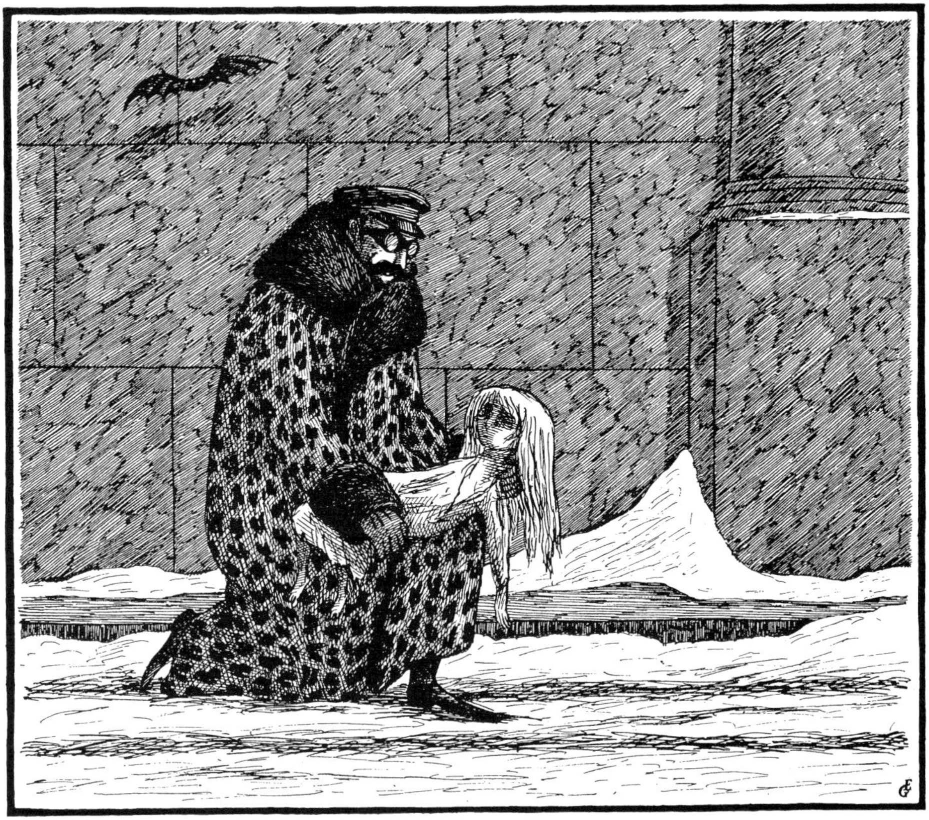

She was so changed, he did not recognize her.

For more Edward Gorey books, puzzles, calendars, games, and stationery, visit pomegranate.com.

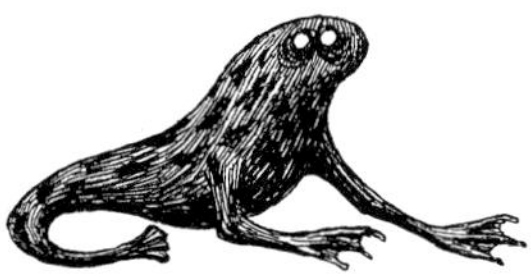

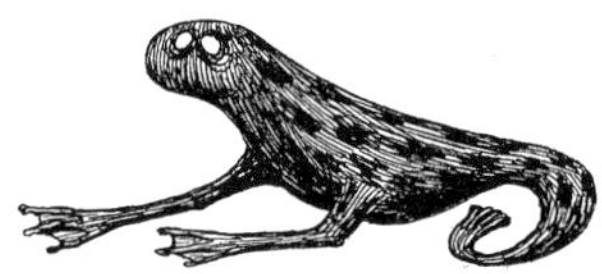

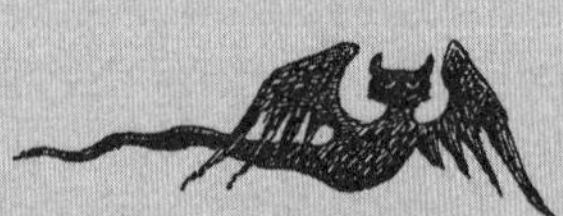